Teachers, librarians, and kids from across Canada had an advance look at *Canadian Flyer Adventures* before publication. Here's what some of them had to say:

Great Canadian historical content, excellent illustrations, and superb closing historical facts (I love the kids' commentary!). ~ SARA S., TEACHER, ONTARIO

As a teacher–librarian I welcome this series with open arms. It fills the gap for Canadian historical adventures at an early reading level! There's fast action, interesting, believable characters, and great historical information. ~ MARGARET L., TEACHER–LIBRARIAN, BRITISH COLUMBIA

The *Canadian Flyer Adventures* will transport young readers to different eras of our past with their appealing topics. Thank goodness there are more artifacts in that old dresser ... they are sure to lead to even more escapades. ~ SALLY B., TEACHER–LIBRARIAN, MANITOBA

When I shared the book with a grade 1–2 teacher at my school, she enjoyed the book, noting that her students would find it appealing because of the action-adventure and short chapters. ~ HEATHER J., TEACHER AND LIBRARIAN, NOVA SCOTIA

Newly independent readers will fly through each *Canadian Flyer Adventure*, and be asking for the next installment! Children will enjoy the fast-paced narrative, the personalities of the main characters, and the drama of the dangerous situations the children find themselves in. ~ PAM L., LIBRARIAN, ONTARIO

I love the fact that these are Canadian adventures—kids should know how exciting Canadian history is. Emily and Matt are regular kids, full of curiosity, and I can see readers relating to them. ~ *JEAN K., TEACHER, ONTARIO*

What kids told us:

I would like to have the chance to ride on a magical sled and have adventures. ~ *EMMANUEL*

I would like to tell the author that her book is amazing, incredible, awesome, and a million times better than any book I've read. ~ *MARIA*

I would recommend the *Canadian Flyer Adventures* series to other kids so they could learn about Canada too. The book is just the right length and hard to put down. ~ *PAUL*

The books I usually read are the full-of-fact encyclopedias. This book is full of interesting ideas that simply grab me. ~ *ELEANOR*

At the end of the book Matt and Emily say they are going on another adventure. I'm very interested in where they are going next! ~ *ALEX*

I like when Emily and Matt fly into the sky on a sled towards a new adventure. I can't wait for the next book! ~ *JI SANG*

Beware, Pirates!

Frieda Wishinsky

Illustrated by Dean Griffiths

MAPLE
TREE
PRESS

Maple Tree Press Inc.
51 Front Street East, Suite 200, Toronto, Ontario M5E 1B3
www.mapletreepress.com

Distributed in Canada by Raincoast Books
9050 Shaughnessy Street, Vancouver, British Columbia V6P 6E5

Distributed in the United States by Publishers Group West
1700 Fourth Street, Berkeley, California 94710

Dedication
For my friend Sheba Meland

Acknowledgements
Many thanks to the hard-working Maple Tree team—Sheba Meland, Anne Shone,
Ann Featherstone, Grenfell Featherstone, Deborah Bjorgan, Cali Hoffman, Erin Walker, and
Dawn Todd—for their insightful comments and steadfast support. Special thanks to Dean
Griffiths and Claudia Dávila for their engaging and energetic illustrations and design.

Cataloguing in Publication Data
Wishinsky, Frieda
Beware, Pirates! / Frieda Wishinsky ; illustrated by Dean Griffiths.

(Canadian flyer adventures ; 1)
ISBN-13: 978-1-897066-79-9 (bound) / ISBN-10: 1-897066-79-1 (bound)
ISBN-13: 978-1-897066-80-5 (pbk.) / ISBN-10: 1-897066-80-5 (pbk.)

1. Frobisher, Martin, Sir, 1535?–1594—Juvenile fiction. I. Griffiths, Dean, 1967– II. Title.
III. Series: Wishinsky, Frieda. Canadian flyer adventures ; v. 1.

PS8595.I834P57 2007   jC813'.54   C2006-904142-3

Design & art direction: Claudia Dávila
Illustrations: Dean Griffiths

We acknowledge the financial support of the Canada Council for the
Arts, the Ontario Arts Council, the Government of Canada through the
Book Publishing Industry Development Program (BPIDP), and the
Government of Ontario through the Ontario Media Development
Corporation's Book Initiative for our publishing activities.

ONTARIO ARTS COUNCIL
CONSEIL DES ARTS DE L'ONTARIO

Printed in Canada
Ancient Forest Friendly: Printed on 100% Post-Consumer Recycled Paper

A   B   C   D   E   F

Contents

1

The Sled

"Do you live here?"

Emily looked up from her sketchbook. A boy was standing in front of her porch. He was tall and skinny. He had curly black hair.

"We just moved in," Emily said. She brushed her long brown bangs out of her eyes. She pushed her red glasses higher up on her nose.

"Is it haunted?" The boy's brown eyes sparkled.

Emily laughed. "I don't think so. But it's old.

No one has lived here for years."

"I saw someone here once," said the boy. "She wore a floppy purple hat."

"That was my Great-Aunt Miranda!" exclaimed Emily. "She was born here in Glenwood. This house belonged to her."

"But why didn't she live here?"

"She travels around the world. She also has an apartment in Paris, France."

"Oh," said the boy. "I live next door. I'm Matt Martinez."

"I'm Emily Bing."

"So, what's it like up there?" asked Matt. He pointed to a small tower on top of the house.

"It's full of old stuff. I've only been up there twice. But Mom said I can play up there any time I want. My bedroom is tiny."

"A tower is more fun than a bedroom any day," said Matt. "I wish we had a tower.

All *we* have is a boring basement."

"Do you want to see it?"

"Awesome!" said Matt. "I'll be right back. I'll tell my mom I'm playing at your house."

As she waited for Matt, Emily finished her sketch of a ship.

"Hey! That's good," said Matt, when he returned. "What kind of ship is it?"

"A pirate ship," said Emily. "I just read a great book about pirates in Canada." She closed her sketchbook and stuck it into her pocket.

"Come on," she said. "Let's go."

Matt followed her up a rickety spiral staircase. The stairs creaked as they climbed.

"It feels spooky already," said Matt.

"It's even spookier in the tower," said Emily.

The tower door was arched like a half-moon. Emily pushed it. It squeaked open.

"Amazing!" said Matt, looking around. He saw a dresser, a rocking chair, lots of boxes, an old wooden trunk, and a tall grandfather clock. "Have you opened the trunk?"

"I did yesterday. It's full of fancy dresses and crazy hats."

"What's in the dresser?"

"I don't know. Let's look."

Emily opened the top drawer of the dresser.

It was filled with rocks, a big hat, a large egg, an old coin, a piece of rope, and lots more. Each object was labelled in old-fashioned handwriting.

Emily picked up the rope. "Wow! It says: *Found on the Aid, a ship from 1577*! I wonder if that was a pirate ship."

"I wish I could talk to a pirate," said Matt. He showed Emily the small digital recorder he always carried in his pocket. "I want to interview people on TV when I grow up."

"I want to be an explorer," said Emily. "I want to travel around the world like Great-Aunt Miranda."

"Is this your great-aunt?" Matt held up a picture from the back of the drawer. The picture showed a girl on a wooden sled.

"It is. Look. Great-Aunt Miranda wrote under the picture."

To Emily,
The sled is yours. Fly it to wonderful adventures.
Love,
Great-Aunt Miranda

6

"What sled? How can a sled fly? What does that mean?" asked Emily.

"Maybe it's a magic sled," said Matt.

Emily laughed. "There's no such thing as a magic sled."

"But there *is* a sled. Right there!" Behind the dresser lay an old red wooden sled with a maple leaf and the words *Canadian Flyer* painted on it.

Emily pulled out the sled. "It doesn't look magic to me," she said.

"Let's sit on it. Maybe something will happen," said Matt.

Emily sat on the front of the sled. Matt hopped in behind her. They waited for something to happen. But nothing did.

"I guess it's just a plain old sled," said Matt.

"No…it's…not," said Emily, her eyes widening. "Wow!"

Shimmery gold words were forming around the maple leaf.

"Awesome!" said Matt.

Emily read the words aloud:

Rub the leaf
Three times fast.
Soon you'll fly
To the past.

"This *is* magic!" said Emily.

"Let's check it out," said Matt.

Emily smiled. "Here goes!" she said. She rubbed the leaf, three times fast!

2

Yikes!

"Emily! I can't see anything!" shouted Matt.

"I can't see either!" shouted Emily. "We're in a fog. What's happening?"

Before Matt could answer, the fog lifted.

"Look!" cried Emily.

They were no longer in the tower. They were no longer in Emily's house. They were no longer in Glenwood.

They were flying.

Emily and Matt grabbed the sides of the sled and held on. They soared higher.

Suddenly they flew into a giant, white cloud. It was so thick, it felt as if they were soaring through whipped cream. Emily couldn't see Matt.

"Matt, are you there?" she called.

"I'm here," he answered. His voice was shaky. "This is definitely spooky."

"This is definitely magic," said Emily.

The sled burst out of the cloud and headed down.

"I see water!" said Emily.

"I see land!" said Matt.

"I see an old wooden sailing ship," said Emily. "Maybe even a pirate ship! Remember the rope I picked up from the dresser? It said, *Found on the Aid, a ship from 1577.*"

"Yikes!" cried Matt.

With a hard thump they landed on the ship's deck. A tall mast with large sails stood in the middle. One smaller mast with sails stood at one end. Another mast stood at the other end. Cannons stuck out from all the sides.

Emily and Matt stood up. They looked at the sled. The magic words were gone.

"Oh no," said Emily. "How will we get back?"

"The magic will take us back," said Matt. "It has to."

Emily and Matt peered around the ship. They saw one man high up on the main mast. Two men snoozed against a big wooden barrel.

"Where's everyone else?" asked Matt.

"Maybe they're still asleep," said Emily.

"But it's daylight," said Matt. Then he looked down. "Emily, look at our clothes!" They were each wearing baggy pants tied below their knees, a shirt tucked into a heavy padded jacket, a belt, and a black cap.

"Where's my recorder?" asked Matt. "These clothes don't have pockets."

"Maybe it's in that pouch on your belt," said Emily, pointing.

Matt looked down. Sure enough, there was a cotton pouch, attached to his belt. The pouch had a drawstring. Matt opened it. "Phew," he said. "It's here."

Emily looked in her pouch. "My sketch-book's here, too. Good old magic."

"Here come more sailors," whispered Matt. "They look like they just woke up."

Emily and Matt hid behind a barrel.

Sailors climbed up from the sleeping quarters below the deck. Some stretched. Others yawned.

Some sailors began to scrub the deck and repair tears in the sails. Others cleaned their long guns.

"The ship must be anchored," whispered Matt. "It's not moving."

Emily and Matt peered over the railing. They weren't far from land. They could see brown hills and patches of ice on the rocky ground.

"Brrr. It's cold," said Emily. She pulled her cap down over her ears. "Let's see what's on the other side of the ship."

She turned and slammed into a tall man.

The man glared at Emily.

"Who are you?" he bellowed. "What are you doing on my ship?" He had piercing eyes, a large moustache, and a pointy beard. A dagger dangled from his waist.

"We're...we're...stowaways," said Emily. "We've run away to see the world."

"And what is that?" said the man, pointing to the sled.

"It's a sled for travelling on snow," said Matt.

"So, you knew we were headed for a land of snow and ice," said the man. "You are spies."

"We're not," said Emily. "We're just kids."

"Why is this the first time I have seen you on my ship?" barked the man.

"We hid," said Emily. "We're very good at hiding. Our parents never find us at home."

"Are you the captain?" asked Matt.

"Of course," snapped the man. "I am Captain Martin Frobisher."

"Wow!" said Emily. "I've heard about you. You're an explorer."

Captain Frobisher's stern face softened. "Then you have surely heard of my exploits in the service of our good Queen Elizabeth."

"Yes," said Emily.

"You know that the Queen personally bid us

farewell before our first expedition in 1576—only one year ago," said Captain Frobisher. "The Queen has great confidence in the success of this, our second expedition."

"I bet she thinks you're really brave to sail so far," said Matt.

"I am honoured by her attention," said the captain. "But enough talk. This ship is no place for useless children."

"We're not useless," protested Emily.

"Silence," growled Captain Frobisher.

Captain Frobisher turned to a group of sailors. "Humphrey, come here," he commanded.

A sailor with a huge stomach and bulging arm muscles hurried over.

"Put them to work," said the captain.

And with that, he stormed off.

3

Biscuits

Humphrey handed them each a bucket of seawater and a pile of rough rags. He told them to scrub until the deck was clean and dry. Humphrey's clothes were torn and dirty. He smelled like sweat and rotten fish.

"I have had my fill of children," he grunted. "For the second day, a boy from these barren lands circles the ship in his boat, looking for his friend. But his friend is our prisoner. And if that boy in the boat dares to step on this ship, I will throw him overboard."

Humphrey grabbed Matt and Emily by their collars. He hoisted them up. "Beware! Your fate may be the same. Now scrub," he snarled. Then he dropped them down hard.

"That hurts," said Emily, straightening up.

"It will hurt more if you do not do as you are told!" shouted Humphrey. "It will hurt like this." Humphrey ran his index finger like a sword across Matt's neck.

"Leave the children alone," said a man. He wore a tight-fitted vest and a white shirt ruffled at the neck. "They mean no harm."

"Only following the captain's orders, sir," muttered Humphrey. Humphrey gave Emily and Matt a menacing look. "I will return," he said. Then he stomped off.

"I am John Mills," said the man. "So you are the two stowaways."

"I'm Emily, and this is Matt. We love adventures."

"This may be more of an adventure than you expected," said John Mills. "The captain is looking for gold. He is certain it lies in the black ore he found on his first expedition."

Gold! thought Emily. *This is real pirate stuff!*

"The captain is also determined to discover what befell five crewmen from the first expedition," said John Mills. "He is sure they were murdered by the people who inhabit this land. The captain will not let the matter rest. I do not know what he will do."

"We'll be careful," Matt assured him.

John Mills smiled. "You are brave, but you must be more than brave. You must be watchful. The captain is known for his temper.

And there are those like Humphrey who do not care if you are only children."

Emily and Matt nodded.

"Meanwhile, you are surely hungry," said John Mills. "In this land of eternal daylight, it is hard to know when to eat."

"Eternal daylight?" asked Emily.

"In the summer months in this northern land, the sun never sets. Wait. I will find some biscuits for you. It is a meagre meal, but it will fill your bellies while you work."

They watched John Mills disappear below deck. Humphrey was eyeing them as he joined the captain at the other end of the ship.

"We'd better look busy," whispered Matt. "At least until John Mills gets back."

Emily dipped a rag into the water. "My teacher, Ms. Stewart, told us that the food on old sailing ships was disgusting," she said.

"They didn't have refrigerators to store food so it went bad. They ate a lot of mouldy biscuits full of bugs called maggots."

"Yuck," said Matt. "I'm not eating anything with bugs."

4

Minik

John Mills handed Emily and Matt each a biscuit. Emily was sure she saw a maggot crawl across its hard, brown surface.

There was no way she was eating it. But what could she tell John Mills? He was kind to them, unlike Captain Frobisher and Humphrey.

"I'm not feeling well," groaned Emily. "My stomach hurts."

"Me too," said Matt, holding his stomach. He moaned. "Ow. Ow."

"Perhaps you still feel the effects of last night's terrible storm," said John Mills gently. "I was certain we would not survive the wind and icy waves. The captain kept us afloat. He never wavers in a storm."

Emily and Matt nodded.

"I must go. I am in charge of the ship while the captain goes ashore in the launch. Beware, children. Many of the crew are nothing more than common pirates like Humphrey."

John Mills left.

"I wish we could get away from Captain Frobisher and Humphrey," said Emily.

"I know. They give me the creeps," said Matt. "Where are we, anyway?"

"I think we're in the Arctic," said Emily. "In a place that was once called Frobisher Bay— after the captain. It's now called Iqaluit. It's the capital of the territory of Nunavut."

"Nunavut," said Matt. "We learned about that in school. It's way up north."

Emily peered over the side of the ship. "Matt, look! Down there."

A boy about their age was bobbing up and down in a large flat-bottomed boat. He wore a sealskin jacket and pants. He waved.

Emily and Matt waved back.

"He must be the boy Humphrey was talking about—the one who's looking for his friend," said Matt. "I bet he heard Humphrey yell at us."

"Everyone heard Humphrey yell at us," said Emily.

"Come," said the boy, pointing to his boat.

"I understand him!" exclaimed Matt. "But he must be speaking the Inuit language. This magic is great."

"Let's go," said Emily. "It will be fun to

explore the shore. But where should we hide the sled?"

Emily and Matt glanced at the sailors. They were busy scrubbing the deck, coiling rope, and polishing their guns.

"There—under that small rowboat," said Matt. "John Mills said they're taking the launch to shore. They're not taking this boat."

Emily and Matt quickly hid the sled under a blanket in the rowboat. Then they told the boy they were ready.

Emily stared at the sea. There were slabs of ice floating around. The boy's boat was close to the side of the ship. But how could they get in without falling into the water? It looked as cold as ice cubes.

"Here," said Matt, as if reading her mind. He picked up a long thick rope from the deck.

"That rope," said Emily in amazement,

"looks just like the one in the dresser."

"You're right!" said Matt. He tied the rope to a hook.

Matt lowered the rope toward the boy. The boy grabbed it and tied it to his boat.

Emily lifted one leg over the railing. She grabbed the rope.

Matt kept his hand on the rope to make sure the knot held. Slowly Emily lowered herself toward the boat. When she reached it, she put one foot in the boat. Then the other. The boat wobbled but the boy kept it steady. Emily scrambled in.

"I made it!"

The boy turned to Emily and smiled. "I am Minik," he said. "My umiak is fast," he said, proudly patting the side of his boat. "It will take us to shore."

"I am Emily and that's Matt."

Matt stared as a large slab of ice bumped against Minik's boat. "Here goes," he said.

He lifted his legs over the railing. He held on tight to the rope. He carefully climbed down, hand over hand. He made it, too.

"We will go now," said Minik. He began to paddle away from the ship.

Emily looked up. She saw Humphrey run to the rail. He was shaking his fist.

"Quick, Matt. Let's hide under this blanket. If Humphrey sees us he'll want to toss us overboard when we come back to get the sled. Then we'll never get out of here alive."

5

Where Are We?

"Stop, boy!" Humphrey yelled at Minik.

Minik ignored him and kept paddling.

"Do you think he saw us?" Matt whispered to Emily.

"I don't know. Let's stay under the blanket until we reach land."

Minik steered the boat between the ice floes. Matt pulled out his recorder.

"Testing. One. Two. Three," he said. "We're hiding under a sealskin blanket in an Inuit boat. The boat looks like it's made of sealskin, too. The year is 1577. We're in the capital of Nunavut. It doesn't look like a capital city. It looks like nobody lives here."

"Minik does," said Emily. "Somewhere."

Minik headed for a small cove. When they were close to land, Minik jumped out into the water. Emily and Matt jumped out, too.

"I feel like a dripping icicle," said Matt, shivering.

Minik tied the umiak to a large jagged rock. "Come," said Minik.

Emily and Matt followed Minik over the hard, rocky ground. Everything was a greyish-brown except for patches of green moss-like plants; there were no trees. And there was no snow on the ground.

They followed Minik over a hill to a flat plain. "This is my home," he said, pointing to a sealskin tent.

Minik entered first. Emily and Matt followed. "These are my friends, Mother," said Minik.

"Welcome," said Minik's mother, smiling warmly. "Sit and eat with us."

Minik's mother offered them a piece of meat. It was raw.

"I feel sick," Matt whispered to Emily.

"Don't worry,' said Emily. "I'll explain."

Emily turned to Minik's mother.

"Thank you," she said. "But we ate a lot this morning." Minik's mother cut a chunk of meat for Minik. He gobbled it down.

"Caribou," he said. "It is good. Perhaps you will eat later."

After Minik finished eating, he stood up. "Come," he said.

They said goodbye to his mother and followed Minik out.

They walked until they reached the bottom of a big hill.

Minik stopped and pointed to the top.

"Look!" said Emily. "It's Captain Frobisher and some other men. That awful Humphrey is there, too."

"But what are they doing?" asked Matt.

The men were piling stones into a high column. When they finished, a trumpeter blasted a few notes. The men knelt down and prayed.

"I bet he's claiming the land for Queen Elizabeth," said Matt.

"But it doesn't belong to the Queen. It belongs to the Inuit people. They were here first," said Emily.

Minik nodded in agreement.

The children hid behind a giant boulder. They watched the captain and his men come down the hill. The Englishmen began walking toward the launch.

Minik pointed to the top of the hill. Some Inuit had climbed up. They were waving at the captain and his men.

The captain and Humphrey stepped away from the rest of the group. Captain Frobisher beckoned the Inuit to come down.

"I wouldn't go if I were them," said Matt.

Minik agreed. "I don't like these men," he whispered. "They took my friend, Irniq."

6

Shot in the Rear

The Inuit signalled to Captain Frobisher in sign language.

"What do they want him to do?" Emily asked Minik.

"They want to trade. They will bring what they have to trade and place it on the ground."

The captain placed some metal bells and a small mirror on the ground. Two of the Inuit put down their bows and arrows and descended the hill carrying a sealskin blanket and jacket. They put their goods on the ground beside the English trinkets. Slowly the Inuit approached Captain Frobisher and Humphrey.

"Why are they doing that?" said Matt.

Minik answered, "To show they are peaceful."

Without warning, the captain and Humphrey grabbed the Inuit and held them down. The Inuit tried to pull free, but they couldn't.

Minik's eyes burned with anger. "These men have no right to hurt my people," he said.

Emily nodded. What was the captain going to do to the Inuit? Did he want to kill them in revenge for the five men who'd disappeared during the last expedition?

The Inuit kicked the captain and Humphrey in the shins. The Englishmen cursed as the Inuit butted them with their heads. The Inuit struggled.

Finally they were free! They ran up the hill and grabbed their bows and arrows. Then they began to shoot at the captain and his companion.

Startled, the Englishmen raced toward the shore. But they weren't fast enough. An arrow hit the captain.

"OW!" he cried.

"Yikes! I think the captain got hit in the rear end," said Emily.

"I bet that hurts," said Matt.

Minik said nothing. He couldn't keep his eyes off the scene.

The captain's men raised their guns and took aim at the Inuit. The deafening sound made the Inuit jump.

They ran, but Humphrey chased after them. He grabbed one of the Inuit and pinned him to the ground. The other Inuit escaped.

"I've got one of them, sir," Humphrey told the captain.

"Do not let him go," said the captain, in a voice weak with pain. "He is our prisoner. He will tell me what happened to my men who disappeared last year. I will not rest until I know their fate."

"You were right," Emily told Minik. "They want to take the Inuit prisoner along with your friend. We have to stop them."

"Yes, but we can do nothing now," said Minik. "Look!" He pointed to the sky. Thick, dark clouds had formed while the men were fighting.

"A storm is coming. We must hurry," said Minik.

7

Storm

Emily, Matt, and Minik ran back toward Minik's tent.

"The English will not be able to reach their ship in time," said Minik.

"They're going to get very cold," said Emily. "And so are we!"

The wind howled like a pack of wolves. The sky grew darker. Ice pellets began to fall. Emily and Matt struggled to keep up with Minik.

"There's the tent!" shouted Emily. They raced inside.

Minik's mother wrapped them all in blankets. They huddled together, trying to get warm and dry.

"The English will be angry at my people for shooting their captain," said Minik. "They may kill the prisoner or bring him to their land." Minik told them about Captain Frobisher's first visit when his crew captured an Inuit man. The Inuit never saw their friend again.

"I want to see Irniq again. I do not want him to die," said Minik. "Can you help me save him?"

"We'll help you," said Emily. "The captain has no right to take him away. I don't care if Captain Frobisher says he's working for the Queen. Captain Frobisher is a brave explorer but he's also a nasty pirate!"

"It's not going to be easy," said Matt. "What if Humphrey saw us go off with Minik in the boat? What if we don't have time to get the sled? Then…" Matt drew his hand across his neck like a sword.

"Maybe the captain and Humphrey aren't back on the ship yet," said Emily.

Emily pulled out her sketchbook. She drew a picture of Minik and his mother.

Matt pulled out his recorder.

"What is that?" asked Minik.

Matt explained that it was something special you talk into. "It's kind of magical," he said. "Here. Listen."

Matt spoke into the recorder. "This is our new friend, Minik. He's very brave."

Minik beamed at Matt's words. And when Matt played back the recording, Minik looked stunned.

8

To the Rescue!

Emily, Matt, and Minik discussed their plan to rescue Irniq.

"When you are on the ship, how will you find Irniq?" asked Minik.

"We'll poke around the ship," said Emily.

"We'll keep looking until we find him," Matt told Minik.

"I will wait for you in my umiak," said Minik.

"Listen," said Matt. "The wind has stopped. I don't hear the rain either."

Minik lifted a flap of the tent. "It looks like the storm is over."

"Let's hurry," said Matt. "Maybe we can beat the captain back to the ship,"

The children thanked Minik's mother and left. She told them to be careful.

As they raced to Minik's umiak, Emily worried about how they'd find Irniq and get him into the boat. And what if the sled wasn't there? How would they get home?

Emily glanced at Matt. He also looked worried. He sounded worried, too. He spoke into his recorder.

"This is Matt reporting from the Arctic. We are on a dangerous mission to help our friend Minik save his friend Irniq from that dastardly pirate Captain Martin Frobisher. They have daggers and guns, and they don't like kids. I hope this will not be my last report."

Matt snapped off his recorder. They had reached the cove where Minik had tied his umiak. The children climbed in.

"Do not fear," Minik reassured them. "We will succeed. We are brave and we are friends."

But despite Minik's words, Emily was afraid their plans might not work. What if Irniq remained a prisoner? What if they became prisoners, too—or worse?

9

I Will Find You

Minik paddled the umiak quickly toward the ship.

"Phew! I don't think the captain made it back yet," said Matt. "The launch isn't here. Maybe the captain's even dead."

"Look!" said Emily. "The sailors are all busy repairing the ship. Wow! The storm really made a mess."

The large sail was ripped and flapping in the wind. Another sail had a big hole in the middle. A wooden barrel was broken, and there were pieces of wood strewn all around the deck.

"Yikes. I hope the rope is still there," said Emily, gulping. "And the rowboat where we hid the sled."

"There's the rope," said Matt. It was frayed but still dangling over the side of the ship. "But I can't see the rowboat!"

Minik paddled close to the side of the ship. He grabbed the rope. "It is strong. I will hold it steady for you. I will keep out of sight until you have found Irniq."

"How will we find you?" asked Matt.

"Do not worry. I will find you," said Minik. "I will stay close to the ship. Then I will paddle to the rope."

Emily grabbed the rope. It was wet from the storm. Her hands slipped and she slid down.

She took a deep breath. Then she grasped

the rope tighter and hoisted herself up. She slid onto the deck.

"Hurry," she whispered to Matt. "Everyone's still busy. The rope is slippery. Hold on tight."

Matt grabbed the rope. He followed Emily up to the deck.

"I will return," said Minik. "All will be well." He paddled away.

"Where should we look for Irniq?" asked Emily.

"Down below," said Matt. He pointed to the ladder leading to the sleeping quarters. The kids bent down low. They ran and hid behind one of the wooden barrels that hadn't broken in the storm. No one paid attention to them.

"Look!" said Matt. "There's the rowboat. It's still in one piece!" They ran and hid behind it.

They were only a few steps away from the ladder.

"Let's go," whispered Matt. They raced to the ladder.

Matt led the way down. "It's dark and spooky down here," he said in a low voice.

"And it smells like a dirty toilet," said Emily, holding her nose.

Two sailors were snoring in their hammocks. Emily and Matt tiptoed past them.

A sailor's pants, shirt, jacket, and dagger lay on the floor. Emily and Matt looked at each other.

Emily picked up the dagger and clothes. She stuffed the clothes under her jacket. "Boy, will I need a shower when I get home," she said.

"We both will," said Matt. They inched their way through the dimly lit cabin. Just as they were about to turn a corner, someone said, "Who goes there?"

Emily and Matt scurried behind a post. It was too late. They were spotted.

"Oh, it is you two," said the voice, laughing. It was John Mills!

"What are you children up to now?" asked John Mills.

"Exploring," said Emily.

"Hmmm. Exploring again," said John Mills. "Now, what do you say about helping me? I have been so busy with the ship's repairs that I have not had time to attend to everything."

"How can we help?" asked Matt.

"There is a young lad in the hold. He has not had anything to eat since the storm. Here is a biscuit. Bring it to him."

"Sure," said Matt. "We'll give it to him."

"He is down there," said John Mills. "Take this candle."

John Mills handed the candle to Emily. "It is very dark, and the rats enjoy dark corners. You will need light."

"Rats?" sputtered Emily.

10

Yo! Ho! Ho!

A boy who looked about twelve was huddled in a corner. He was tied by a rope to a hook on the wall.

"Minik sent us to help you," whispered Matt.

A smile spread across Irniq's face when he heard his friend's name.

"We have to untie him," said Emily.

"I'll cut the rope with the dagger," said Matt.

Emily handed him the dagger. A large rat scampered across the floor.

Matt shuddered. Then he began slicing away at the rope binding Irniq's hands.

"Hurry," said Emily. "I don't hear the sailors snoring any more."

"I'm trying," said Matt. "But the ropes are tight."

Matt kept slicing. The children could hear voices close by. They couldn't make out the words.

Emily's stomach twisted into a knot. Who was talking? Were the captain and Humphrey back?

"Done," said Matt. Irniq was free!

"Shh. I hear footsteps," said Emily.

The children didn't move. The footsteps sounded like they were going up the ladder.

"I think the sailors have gone up on deck," said Matt.

"Here, put these on," Emily told Irniq.

She pulled the sailor's clothes out from under her jacket. "And here's my cap," said Matt. "Pull it over your face. Hurry. Let's go."

Emily blew the candle out. The children and Irniq tiptoed through the sleeping quarters.

It was quiet. No one seemed to be below the deck but them.

"I'll peek out and see if the coast is clear," said Emily.

They climbed up the ladder and Emily looked around. The sailors were all busy repairing the large sail.

"Let's get the sled," Emily whispered.

Irniq and Matt followed Emily up the stairs. They hurried toward the rowboat. They lifted the blanket.

Phew! The sled was there. They lifted it up and rushed to the rope-end at the railing to look for Minik.

Before they reached it, a sailor stumbled into Matt.

"Who are you?" mumbled the sailor, tottering around.

"My name is Matt," said Matt. "We're helping around the ship."

"Carry on," said the sailor. "I will rest right here. My head feels like it is on fire."

The sailor slumped against the railing.

He slid down the railing and onto the deck. In an instant, he was sound asleep.

"He's totally drunk," said Emily.

"Yo! Ho! Ho! And a bottle of rum," said Matt, laughing. He peered over the railing. "Look! There's Minik."

Minik steered closer to the railing. He grabbed the rope. He steadied it as Irniq lifted his leg over the railing and lowered himself down into the boat. Just as Irniq sat down, someone on board cried out. Matt and Emily spun around.

"Stop, you scoundrels!" shouted the captain, hobbling toward them. He shook his fist.

Behind him, Humphrey pulled out his dagger. He pointed it at the children.

"Quick!" cried Matt. "Jump on the sled!"

Emily slid onto the sled. Matt hopped on in front.

But there were no magic words on the sled. The captain and Humphrey were coming closer and closer. They were about to grab the children when the shimmery gold words suddenly appeared:

You've done your best.
You've helped a friend.
Say: "Sled, go home."
It's journey's end.

"Sled, go home!" hollered Matt.

They rose in the air.

The captain and Humphrey cursed.

John Mills ran to the captain's side. He looked stunned as he stared at the sled. Then he smiled and tipped his hat.

Matt and Emily rose higher. As the sled turned, they saw Minik's umiak touch the shore.

Then Matt and Emily sailed into the giant, white cloud, leaving the *Aid* far below.

Soon they were back in Emily's tower. Matt checked the clock. It was 11:00 a.m.—the same time as when they had left. Time had stood still!

"That was awesome!" said Matt. "I can't believe we went back in time!"

"And we weren't even tossed overboard," said Emily.

"But we almost were."

"Almost doesn't count," said Emily, laughing.

"It's funny now, but it didn't feel funny then," said Matt. "It felt…"

"Scary but fun," said Emily. "I wonder if Great-Aunt Miranda travelled to pirate times."

"If she did, she must have touched one of the objects in the dresser first, like we did. And if we're going on another adventure, we'll have to touch a different object, like…that dinosaur egg."

"So, when do you want to go on another adventure?" asked Emily.

"Soon—just not today. I'm starving."

"Do you want to stay for lunch? We're having biscuit sandwiches and seaweed salad."

"You are not!" said Matt.

Emily laughed. "We're not! We're having tuna."

MORE ABOUT...

After their adventure, Emily and Matt wanted to know more about pirates and the Inuit. Turn the page for their favourite facts.

Emily's Top Ten Facts

1. The Inuit have lived in the Arctic for over 6,000 years.

2. The land in Nunavut is frozen and there are no trees. This kind of land is called tundra.

3. In the summer, the top of the soil in Nunavut thaws out. Plants, like lichen, moss, shrubs, and grasses, grow.

4. On a map, Nunavut looks like an inukshuk. An inukshuk is a pile of stones, sometimes shaped like a person, that helps guide people across the Arctic.

5. It's an Inuit tradition to catch fish and birds, and to harpoon seals and whales in the spring. In summer the Inuit have hunted caribou and musk oxen. In winter, they've caught seals through the ice.

6. The Inuit traded with Norsemen from Greenland over 1,000 years ago—500 years before Martin Frobisher was born.

7. Martin Frobisher was terrible at spelling and could barely read.

He was good at yelling though. —M.

8. When he started out as a pirate, Martin Frobisher was arrested four times, but he was always let go.

He was good at getting in and out of trouble, too! —M.

9. The sailors with Martin Frobisher saw a big fish with a horn and thought it was a sea unicorn. (It was probably a narwhal.)

10. In 1993, over four hundred years after Martin Frobisher sailed into the Arctic, Nunavut became a territory of Canada. Nunavut means "Our Land" in the Inuit language, Inuktitut.

Matt's Top Ten Facts

1. This is what Martin Frobisher took on the Aid:
Forty bushels of dried
peas, oatmeal, rice, salt, dried
beef, bacon, forty tons of
biscuits, barrels of flour,
vinegar, oil, and butter.

They didn't take any real cookies. They would have had a lot more fun if they did! -E.

2. Scurvy, a sickness you get when you don't have enough vitamin C, killed many pirates.

3. Pirate ships were full of rats. Rats carried diseases that also killed lots of pirates.

4. More pirates died of disease than by swords or bullets.

5. When butter went bad on an old sailing ship, they used it to grease pulleys.

6. When cheese went bad it was sometimes shaped into buttons for sailor's clothes.

7. If you flew the Jolly Roger, a black flag with a white skull and crossbones, you most likely were a pirate.

Maybe Humphrey smelled because his buttons were made of mouldy cheese! Or maybe it's that he just hadn't taken a bath in months. -E.

8. Pirates flogged (beat) their crew or captives but almost no one actually walked the plank—except in the movies.

9. If you were caught as a pirate, you were sometimes hanged or put in prison. Floating prisons on ships were some of the worst places to be sent.

10. Even though Martin Frobisher never found real gold, he was knighted in 1588 by the Queen for fighting the Spanish Armada.

So You Want to Know...

From Author Frieda Wishinsky

When I was writing this book, my friends wanted to know more about Martin Frobisher and the story I wrote. I told them that *Beware, Pirates!* is based on historical facts and Martin Frobisher was a real privateer. I did make up many of the other characters, though, like Humphrey and John Mills. I also told them this:

What kind of pirate was Martin Frobisher?

He was a privateer. Some explorers were also privateers, who looted enemy ships for Queen Elizabeth I of England. She gave her privateers a license and called them "sea dogs."

What other privateers worked for the Queen?

Two other famous explorers, Sir Walter Raleigh and Sir Francis Drake, were also privateers working for Queen Elizabeth. They attacked Spanish ships, and they explored new lands, looking for riches.

Why did Frobisher become a privateer?

Although Frobisher was born into a well-to-do family (in 1539), he wasn't a good student. He was also hot-tempered, and he lacked social graces. His family was sure he wouldn't be successful at business or government so they sent him out to sea.

What were his first adventures like at sea?

At 14, he was one of the lucky survivors of an expedition to Africa. The next year, he was held hostage for months by an African chief. Frobisher kept being imprisoned and released. He realized that to stay out of jail and make money, his best bet was to offer his services to the Queen as a privateer.

Did Frobisher like being a pirate?

He liked navigation. He liked capturing ships and looting. He liked being in charge. Yes! I'd say he liked being a pirate.

Did the Queen like Frobisher?

At first she didn't trust him, until Frobisher convinced her that he could find the fabled Northwest Passage that linked the Atlantic to the Pacific. People thought that was the route to the riches of China. And after Frobisher's first expedition to the Arctic, when he thought he found gold, the Queen appreciated him even more!

Did Frobisher really take captives?

On his first expedition, he kidnapped an Inuit man and brought him back to England. The man soon became sick and died. On Frobisher's second expedition (the one mentioned in *Beware, Pirates!*), he kidnapped an Inuit man, woman, and child. They also fell ill and died in England.

Was Frobisher really mean and angry?

Like a lot of pirates, he could be cruel if he was disobeyed. But he was also brave. He dove into icy water to rescue drowning sailors.

Did Frobisher go on a third expedition?

Yes. Even though the ore he brought back on his second expedition proved worthless, he sailed off to the Arctic again. This time he took 15 ships and brought back 1,110 tons of ore. But it was all just worthless rocks—again!

What did he do next?

After three failed expeditions, Frobisher had enough of exploring and searching for gold. He continued to fight for the Queen, though, by attacking Spanish ships (Spain was an enemy of England at the time). He died after being wounded fighting the Spanish on November 22, 1594.

Send In Your
Top Ten Facts

If you enjoyed this adventure as much as Matt and Emily did, maybe you'd like to collect your own facts about pirates, Martin Frobisher, and the Inuit, too.

Email in your favourite facts to CFATopTen@mapletreepress.com. Maple Tree Press will choose the very best facts that are sent in to make a *Canadian Flyer Adventures* Readers' Top Ten Facts for *Beware, Pirates!*

Each reader who sends in a fact that is selected for the final Top Ten will receive a new book in the *Canadian Flyer Adventures* series! (If more than one person sends in the same fact and it is chosen, the first person to submit that fact will be the winner.)

We look forward to hearing from you!

Coming next in the
Canadian Flyer Adventures Series…

Canadian Flyer Adventures
#2

Danger,
Dinosaurs!

Turn the page for a sneak peek.

From *Danger, Dinosaurs!*

The sun beat down on their heads, arms, and legs. There were few trees along the way to give them shade.

"There has to be a pond, or a brook, or even a puddle somewhere," said Emily, wiping sweat out of her eyes.

Matt pointed ahead. "I think I see something over there."

"I hope you're right," said Emily. "I'm so thirsty that I could drink a whole pond by myself."

Emily and Matt kept walking.

"It is a pond. I'm sure of it!" cried Matt as they neared the spot he'd seen.

Emily ran toward the pond. Matt followed

with the sled. Tall grass encircled the pond.

Emily bent over and cupped the water into her hands. "This is the most delicious water that I've tasted in my whole life," she declared.

Matt slurped a handful. "Awesome!" he said.

Emily sat up and stared at the pond. "It's so hot. I wish we could swim."

"Why can't we?" said Matt. "The pond is shallow. I can see down to the bottom everywhere."

"But we don't have bathing suits."

"Who needs bathing suits? We can swim in our clothes. It's so hot, they'll dry in no time," said Matt.

"So," said Emily.

"So," said Matt.

"So, let's do it!" they said together.

Emily and Matt took off their shoes and

socks. Emily took her sketchbook out of her pocket and Matt took his recorder out of his pocket. They placed everything beside the sled on the grass. "It will be hidden and safe here," said Matt.

"One...two...three...in!" they sang.

The water was cool but not icy. The pond was shallow. They could touch bottom everywhere with their feet.

Emily and Matt splashed water at each other.

"This is great," said Matt. "The sky is blue. The water feels good. So, what do you think of dinosaur times now?"

"I...I...think we're not alone," stammered Emily. "I hear something."

Matt looked up. Six huge eyes stared at them.

The *Canadian Flyer Adventures* Series

Upcoming Books

Look out for these new books that take Emily and Matt on new adventures.

#2 Danger, Dinosaurs!
#3 Crazy for Gold

And more to come!

About the Author

Frieda Wishinsky, a former teacher, is an award-winning picture- and chapter-book author, who has written many beloved and bestselling books for children. Frieda enjoys using humour and history in her work, while exploring new ways to tell a story. Her books have earned much critical praise, including a nomination for a Governor General's Award in 1999. In addition to the books in the *Canadian Flyer Adventures* series, Frieda has published *What's the Matter with Albert?*, *A Quest in Time*, and *Manya's Dream* with Maple Tree Press. Frieda lives in Toronto.

About the Illustrator

Gordon Dean Griffiths realized his love for drawing very early in life. At the age of 12, halfway through a comic book, Dean decided that he wanted to become a comic book artist and spent every spare minute of the next few years perfecting his art. In 1995 Dean illustrated his first children's book, *The Patchwork House*, written by Sally Fitz-Gibbon. Since then he has happily illustrated over a dozen other books for young people and is currently working on several more, including the *Canadian Flyer Adventures* series. Dean lives in Duncan, B.C.